A DRINK OF WATER

A Drink of Water

And Other Stories

JOHN YEOMAN

illustrated by

QUENTIN BLAKE

Thames & Hudson

CONTENTS

PUBLISHER'S NOTE

It's a huge privilege to introduce to a new generation of readers this first collaboration between John Yeoman and Quentin Blake, who have gone on to make so many wonderful and memorable books together in the decades since this was first published. It is also the very first book illustrated by Quentin Blake, whose influence on contemporary illustration is without parallel. *A Drink of Water* is a joy to publish, and I know you'll find it a joy to read too.

Roger Thorp

FOREWORD

When I started out as a freelance illustrator in the late 1950s I worked for a variety of magazines, but what I most wanted to do was the complete illustration of a whole book within its own covers. I really had no idea how to set about this, so I asked my friend John Yeoman if he could write something for me. He produced a collection of stories, based on the folktales of various countries and retold in his own idiom. We offered them to the publisher Faber and Faber, who published *A Drink of Water* in 1960.

It was the first book I had illustrated, and our first book together. It was not unsuccessful, but has been out of print for probably fifty years, and it's impossible to buy a copy. Now Thames & Hudson, in partnership with the House of Illustration, are generously publishing this facsimile edition. Apart from this page of explanation, the words and pictures you have in your hand are exactly as they were on the first day of their publication.

Quentin Blake

A DRINK OF WATER

It was a terribly hot day in the jungle, and all the birds and beasts, exhausted from the heat, had curled up to sleep. The silence was broken only by an occasional snapping of twigs and beating of soft-feathered wings as a parrot nearly slipped off its perch in a tall tree.

The only creature who couldn't sleep was a small brown monkey, who was very very thirsty indeed. He wandered on all fours through the lush green undergrowth in the hope of finding a small puddle. Every now and then he stopped and raised himself on to his back legs, peering this way and that for a tell-tale sparkle of sunlight on water. But it was useless, for it had been a very very long, hot, dry summer.

At last his search led him to the edge of the dark green jungle, to the place where the desert begins. He stopped again, blinking into the strong sunlight. But he knew that there was no chance at all of finding cool water in the desert.

But what was that he could see? Out there, standing all by itself, was a tall, fat pot—just the sort of pot which might be expected to have water in it. With a bound the monkey was beside it. If he climbed on to a dead branch among the stones he could just manage to peer into the dark inside of the pot. Was there water in it? He couldn't see any water, but then, it was very dark in there. Gingerly he lowered a thin arm into the pot. His long sensitive fingers could feel a coolness which might mean that there was water further down. So he very carefully lowered his hand further, and further, and further until he was standing on tiptoe and his arm was stretched as far as it would go. And then the very tips of his long fingers felt cold water.

And now what was he to do, may I ask? Just think, the water was so near, and yet so hard to reach!

"I will put my shoulder to the pot," said the small brown monkey, gently scratching his lower lip with a long finger, "and I will rock it until it tumbles over—and then I will drink the water." And he put his thin bony shoulder against the pot, and pushed with all his might. Then he pushed again and again and again until—the pot began to rock. It rocked very little at first but gradually it swayed more and more and it seemed that the very next push would send it toppling over.

"Stop!" called a small voice. The small brown monkey stopped in surprise, and the pot gently rocked itself to a standstill. There was no-one to be seen.

"Who said that?" asked the small brown monkey.

"I did," said a green lizard, sliding quickly from beneath the pot and raising his head towards the monkey. "I live under this pot and I was trying to have a nap when you came and started making the ground shake. And why are you wearing that fur on a hot day like this?"

The monkey did not answer the last question and looked very ashamed.

"I am sorry to disturb you," he said, "but I wanted to drink that cool water. I can't reach it and so I must spill it on the ground before I can drink it."

"Really, you ought to have more sense," said the lizard. "Just look at the ground." And he whisked round in a flash, so that one moment he was facing one way and the next he was facing the other. "It's all hot stone and dry dust," he went on. "If you spill the water then the ground will drink it all up before you could get a single drop. Think of something else and have the goodness to make less noise about it when other people are sleeping." And with that he darted under the pot once more.

The small brown monkey sat down on the stones of the desert and looked at the pot again, and felt thirstier than ever.

He had been sitting for a few minutes with the sun beating down on him, when suddenly he felt cold. He noticed that he was now sitting in shadow, and looking up he saw a great black shape hovering over him.

"Who's that?" asked the monkey.

"I am a monkey-eating eagle," said the big shape, coming nearer, "and who are you?"

Now the small brown monkey knew what was good for him, and fortunately he was clever enough to have an answer ready. "By a strange coincidence," he replied quickly, "I am an eagle-eating monkey, and I should be pleased to meet you."

The big bird hastily rose several feet higher into the blue sky.

"Have you by any chance," called the small brown monkey after him, "seen any water about in your travels?"

"From up here I can see everything," came the reply, "and the only water that I can see is the hippopotamus's pond." With that the great bird rose higher still. "Second on the left

past the mango tree and first right after the paw-paw tree."
And with that the great bird soared up and up until it disappeared into the sky.

It was a hot and thirsty little monkey who trudged back into the stuffy green heat of the jungle. He followed the direction given to him, and at last arrived at the hippopotamus's pond. But what a disappointment awaited him! Instead of cool, fresh water, as he had hoped, there was thick, steaming, muddy water.

"Ugh! I can't drink that!" said the sad creature, and he squatted down on his hind quarters and cried.

Now the hippopotamus had seen and heard all this from her position in the middle of the pool. But because she was almost completely under the water (all except her eyes and her nostrils) the monkey hadn't noticed her. At first she had kept quite still because she had been a little offended—I may as well admit it—by the monkey's unwillingness to drink her beautiful bathwater. However, she was a tender-hearted old thing and as soon as the monkey began to cry, she floated to the surface and, garlanded with smelly pond-weed, swam to the bank.

"There, there," she said comfortingly. "Did you want a drink, then?"

The monkey looked up quickly and gazed at the large smiling face which greeted him. In fact, he rather forgot his manners and *stared* at it, fascinated by the bristles on her chin. But he quickly remembered himself and said, "Good afternoon. Yes, I would very much like a drink, because I'm so hot and thirsty."

"Then just wait for me to climb out and I'll help you search through the jungle for water," said the hippopotamus.

It was such a well-meant and kind offer that the monkey felt he had to accept it, although he knew that apart from the water in the pot, which he couldn't reach, there wasn't a single drop in the whole jungle.

So he waited for the hippopotamus to come out of the pond—and she did. And what do you think! The monkey noticed, with his eyes wide open with delight, that as she climbed out of the pond, the level of the water slowly went down.

"Oh, please get in again!" called the monkey excitedly.

"But I want to help you," insisted the hippopotamus.

"And so you will!" cried the small brown monkey.

With a puzzled look on her huge face, but nevertheless pleased to be useful, the hippopotamus sank slowly back into the water. Sure enough, as she did so the water rose again in the pond.

"Hurrah!" shouted the monkey, bounding away. Then, remembering his manners again, he bounded back and said quietly, "Thank you very much for helping me. I am most grateful to you." And he ran off to the edge of the jungle.

Back at the pot he quickly collected an armful of big stones—the biggest he could find. He carried them to the side of the pot, climbed up on to the branch, and began to drop the stones in, ever so gently, one by one.

"Splash!" went the first one, faintly, as it hit the bottom.

"Splash!" went the next, a little louder.

And he dropped in more and more until the big pot was three-quarters filled with stones and—what do you think?—the water had risen to the very brim. All the monkey had to do then was to purse his lips and drink the fresh, cool water from the top of the pot.

"And when the water gets too low again," he said happily to himself, "I can always drop some more stones in."

It's a clever monkey who uses his eyes and his common-sense.

Story Two

THE DOG AND THE BEAR

O ne day a peasant said to his dog, "You are getting too old and lazy to guard my chickens and my house. I will buy myself a new dog, a young dog, and you can go off to the forest to live, for I am not going to feed you any longer."

And so the poor old dog, who had been very faithful to his master, went sadly into the forest. He had always had his food and drink put down for him in little enamel bowls and after hours of searching could not find anything to eat in the forest.

At last a kindly bear ambled past.

"Please, bear, I have been turned out into the dark forest to find my own food, and there seems to be nothing to eat here at all."

The bear was very sorry for the poor dog and offered him a bees' nest. "Have some honey," he said. "It's good for the voice."

The dog gratefully thrust his tongue into the nest, but all the honey got up his nose and made him sneeze. "I don't think dogs eat honey," he said miserably. "Haven't you any meat?"

The bear hadn't any meat, but he said that if the dog would like to be his partner, between them they could have all the meat they wanted. The dog would have to do the hunting and the bear, who was as strong as any animal in the forest, would do the killing. But both agreed that this would be hard work.

Suddenly the bear sat up with a look of triumph on his face. "I have a wonderful idea," he said. "We will go to your old master's house and I will creep up to the cot that stands on the porch and snatch the baby from it. Then you will chase me and I will pretend to be frightened and run away. When you return the baby to its parents, they will be so grateful that you will get your old job back again."

"It sounds better than working for a living," said the dog. "But what do you get out of it?"

The bear looked wise and said, "I'll scratch your back, you scratch mine." So the dog scratched the bear's broad back, although he still did not understand how the plan would help the bear.

Next day the huge bear tiptoed up to the baby's cot, lifted the baby gently in his great paws and stuck his head in at the window of the house, making a fearful roar as he did so. The mother screamed and rushed out, waving a broom. But the bear lumbered off, faster than she could run. The new dog was afraid of such a big, fierce animal, and he would not come out of his kennel. But our dog, waiting for the right moment, ran from behind the house, barking for all he was worth, and caught up with the bear. The bear stopped in his tracks, laid the baby carefully on the ground, rose awkwardly on his back legs, raised his arms above his head, and said, "Heaven save us—a dog!" Then he shuffled away while dog took the baby back to its mother. When her husband came in from the fields he said, "I was wrong. There is life in the old dog yet. He shall have his job back again."

Once more the dog was given all the food and drink he wanted in enamel bowls. One day, when he was lazing in the sun with one eye on the chickens, the bear appeared.

"Now," said the bear, "it is your turn to help me. Your master and his wife are giving a party to a few of their friends in there, and you must invite me in, too."

"I can't," said the dog, "for someone would be sure to see you."

"I will sit at the back," said the bear.

So they went into the house very quietly, without anyone noticing, and the bear sat on a chair behind everyone else, in a dark corner. Everybody was so busy talking and eating and drinking that they did not bother to look round at him, although from time to time they passed him cups of tea and fancy iced pastries over their shoulders.

But at last the guests began to sing songs, clapping their hands to the music, and this was too much for the bear. He loved singing, and could not help joining in. The louder the guests sang, the louder he sang (but not the same song, because he only knew bear songs). In the end he was so excited that he was lifting his knees and pounding his feet on the floor.

"Fmoo, fmoo!" he roared at the top of his voice, which, as you know, is bear singing. Suddenly, too suddenly for the bear, the guests finished their song, only to be amazed by the row coming from the dark corner.

"It's a bear!" cried someone. "The same bear!" cried someone else. "That dog brought him in!" they all screamed. "They must have been friends all the time!" And they all got brooms and shovels and mops and sticks and chased the bear and the dog back into the forest.

In the forest they were kept very busy in their search for food, although they still had time enough to scratch each other's back occasionally.

THE DISCONTENTED
JACKDAW

There was once a young jackdaw who lived under the eaves of a little village church. He was a handsome fellow with his glossy black feathers, gray cap and clear blue eyes, and he would sit for hours nattering to himself while he ran his beak through each sleek feather in turn until he was satisfied that he was looking smarter than any of the other jackdaws.

One bright, sunny afternoon when the air was filled with the smell of cut grass, the young jackdaw thought that it would be a good idea to take a turn about. This was partly because it was such a beautiful day and partly because he had spent an extra long time over his preening and wanted to show the other jackdaws how fine he was looking. So gently, very gently, he dropped from his perch on the weather vane of the church, and spreading wide his wings sank down towards the ground. As he passed the other jackdaws, who were all wheeling playfully around the church spire, the young bird called to them. Of course, they all turned to look at him as he sailed past.

"How smart he looks today," said one jackdaw.

"Finer than ever," replied another. And all the other jackdaws in their turn complimented their young friend.

Pleased that everyone admired his appearance, the young jackdaw let himself drop into a gentle current of air which lifted him easily up the side of the spire to where the other jackdaws were playing. The young jackdaw joined in the game, turning this way and that, gliding effortlessly about the church. And all the time he was thinking, "Oh, what a smart fellow I must be. Everybody says so. I must be the smartest bird in the whole of our family. Those rooks and crows and ravens are so ragged and untidy."

Pleased with this thought and happy to feel the warm sun on his back and the cool breeze on his face, the jackdaw swung easily through the air and made his way towards a nearby wood. Down he came, swerving among the trees and bushes to give the other birds a chance to see what a dapper little jackdaw he was. He weaved in and out of the tree-trunks until at last he met a sight which quite took his breath away.

There, in front of him, perched over a nest on a branch and holding in its beak a wonderful sky-blue egg with black spots on it, sat the most beautiful bird that the jackdaw had ever seen. For after all, he had spent all his time near the little church and had only seen birds like sparrows, pigeons, rooks, crows, ravens and other jackdaws. Now all of these are very pretty in their way, but this bird that was sitting in front of him at this very minute, hastily replacing the egg in the nest, this bird was quite different. This bird was colored, beautifully colored. Reddish-brown above and pinkish-brown below, with black and white stripes on his head and blue and white stripes on his wings, this was surely the most handsome bird that ever was.

"Er ... how do you do?" said the bird, and a rather guilty smile appeared on its beak. "I was just looking after these eggs while the thrushes are away," he explained. "Keeping an eye on them to see that they don't get too cold, you know. They need turning over from time to time. Didn't notice you there at first, you gave me quite a start. So sorry to have kept you." The bird spoke a trifle quickly, and for all his politeness he sounded just a little impatient.

"But you haven't kept me," said the jackdaw. And then, "You *are* a fine bird. Please, sir, what are you called and which family do you belong to?"

"I am a jay," replied the bird, "and I belong to the crow family. And ... oh, these poor eggs." Having said this he looked quickly from side to side, and turned the eggs over lovingly with his beak.

A crow. The jackdaw could hardly believe that a crow could wear such beautiful feathers. His little heart beat faster as he asked, "Do you think you could spare one or two of your colored feathers for me? One or two small ones?"

The jay, to his surprise, eagerly plucked out one tuft of red-brown and one tuft of blue-and-white feathers and offered them to the jackdaw.

"There we are, young fellow. I expect you'll want to be flying off to your friends now. So good-bye," said the jay.

The jackdaw took the feathers, sticking the red-brown ones into his own feathers on his back and the blue-and-white ones into his wings. And then, for fear that the kind jay should change his mind, the young jackdaw said a quick "Thank you" and flew farther into the wood.

How the other jackdaws would admire him. If they thought him handsome before, what would they think now? His daydreams were suddenly interrupted by a rat-a-tat-tat noise from a nearby tree. Out of curiosity he landed on a branch (with difficulty, as his new feathers were upsetting his sense of balance a little). And there, in front of him, was a sight which quite took his breath away. Sitting on the side of a tree—yes, on the side—was a wonderful bird with a red head and a body all yellow and green. He was making a rat-a-tat-tat noise by drumming his beak on the trunk of the tree in front of him.

"How exquisite!" thought the jackdaw. "I must introduce myself, and then perhaps he too will let me have a few feathers to wear."

And so the jackdaw jumped, rather awkwardly, from his branch and landed on the other tree next to the new bird. But partly because his jay's feathers made him heavier than usual, and partly because Nature didn't intend jackdaws to walk up the sides of trees, the young bird found the greatest difficulty in holding on, and at last, after scraping frantically with his feet against the bark of the tree, he fell plop! in a soft feathered heap on to the ground.

"All right?" asked the other bird kindly, without stopping his rat-a-tat-tatting.

"Yes, I think so, sir," replied the jackdaw, feeling carefully with his beak for any broken bones. "Yes, quite all right, thank you."

"Good," said the other bird, "and did you want anything?"

The jackdaw gazed up eagerly. "I only wanted to tell you what a handsome bird I think you are, handsomer even than the jay, and to ask you if you could spare a few, just a few, of your beautiful feathers for me." He was overjoyed when the woodpecker, for that was what the bird was, said, "With pleasure." At least the jackdaw thought that he must have said that, but his head was vibrating so quickly and the noise of the rat-a-tat-tatting was so loud that it was very difficult to catch what he said. In any case, without looking down for a moment to where the jackdaw sat, the woodpecker shook loose from himself a little shower of red, yellow and green feathers which the jackdaw ran about collecting at the foot of the tree.

In no time the jackdaw had stuck all the new feathers into his own, and saying "Thank you" to the woodpecker, he strutted off through the undergrowth. And a strange little creature he looked too, all black and brown and red and green and blue and white and yellow. He was just thinking to himself that he could never have looked as fine as this before or felt as happy as this before when he stopped in amazement. For there, in front of him, was a sight which quite took his breath away.

It was a bird, the biggest bird that he had ever seen. And it stood among the bracken, all shining with green and purple and bronze, with the longest and the most elegantly tapering tail that you could imagine. The bird spoke to the jackdaw first. "Excuse me," he said in a very friendly and confidental voice, "I hope you don't mind my pointing this out, but you have some black on your face. Please don't be offended, but I thought you'd like to know."

It was meant kindly, of course, but I'm afraid that the poor little jackdaw was rather hurt by this remark. His only wish now was to cover himself completely with borrowed feathers,

feathers as beautiful as those which these strange new birds of the woods all wore.

"Thank you very much for telling me, Mr. er ..."

"Pheasant."

"Pheasant," he said. "Yes, I know that I have got rather dusty walking through the wood. Would it be asking you too much of a favor to give me a few of your bright feathers to wear for the time being?"

The pheasant was only too pleased to be able to help and gladly plucked out a whole beakful of his own glistening, colored feathers. Catching sight of an exposed bit of jackdaw at the back, without a word the pheasant removed two of its beautiful tail feathers and handed them too to the excited young bird. They were soon in place and the jackdaw couldn't say "Thank you" enough before half waddling, half hopping away through the undergrowth once more.

This time his path led him down towards the river where the rushes grow thick. And he hadn't gone far before he saw a sight which took his breath away. There, standing before him, unaware of his presence, was a tall bird with the most beautiful speckly brown-and-white breast. Just what the jackdaw needed to put the finishing touch to his new costume.

At last the bird caught sight of him, gave a little scream and stood bolt upright, straining its beak into the air. The jackdaw looked up in the same direction expecting to see something, but there was only deep blue sky and billowing cloud. The strange bird's heart was beating visibly beneath the wonderful pattern on its breast and it seemed to be terribly nervous about something.

The jackdaw spoke to it, "Please, sir," he said, "there is nothing to be alarmed at. I am only a jackdaw."

"Huh. A likely story. I know better," said the other bird in a shaking, strangled voice, and still not changing its erect position. "Jackdaws are black, and you are red and green and blue and copper and ..."

"Well, I *was* a jackdaw, but now I am partly a woodpecker, partly a jay, partly ..."

"I wasn't born yesterday," said the other, still very frightened. "I know the rules. We have a saying, 'Once a bittern ...'"

"Twice shy?"

"'Always a bittern'," continued the other, ignoring the jackdaw's interruption. "And as sure as I'm a bittern, you are no jackdaw. I don't know what you are, but I don't like this business, and whatever you say you needn't think that I'm going to come out of hiding."

"But what's the matter?" asked the jackdaw. "Why are you talking out of the corner of your beak?"

"After all, there aren't many of us left now ..." continued the bittern, who seemed to be talking to himself.

It was clear to the jackdaw that there was no sense to be got out of the bittern, and so very gently he removed a few feathers from the speckly breast and crept quietly away, leaving the bittern standing upright and trembling among the rushes.

Weighed down as he was by all the new feathers which by now covered him completely, it took the jackdaw a long time to walk back to his church beyond the wood. At last he arrived, footsore and exhausted, with just enough strength left

* *

in him to be able to call out to the other jackdaws, "Just come down here and look at me. Just see what *I'm* wearing."

Hearing the call, the other jackdaws flocked down to inspect, and what a sight met their eyes! In a little bedraggled heap of colored feathers, none of which fitted very well and most of which were working loose after the long journey, sat the young jackdaw. But the other jackdaws couldn't recognize him any more.

"It's a sort of parrot," they said.

"No," said the young jackdaw proudly, "I am a ..."

"Scrag him, chaps," someone cried. "It's a sort of parrot!" And all at once the jackdaws hurled themselves upon the unfortunate youngster, pecking at his bright feathers and scolding angrily. Then they rose up together and soared towards the spire where they continued to scold as they wheeled about.

When the little cloud of brightly colored feathers settled once more, there was the jackdaw, sitting sadly on the ground, the twinkle gone from his blue eye.

"I have learnt my lesson," he said. "It is far better to be a smart black jackdaw than a brightly colored make-believe bird."

And it was a sadder but wiser young jackdaw who flew up to join his companions in their never-ending game around the church spire.

THE EWE AND THE NANNY GOAT

Once upon a time, a long way from here, there lived a ewe and a nanny-goat in a small farmyard. They were both rather elderly and they both shared the very same wish—that one day they would be able to pack their things and go out into the wide world in search of adventure. You see, they had spent their lives in that small farmyard. Every day for as long as they could remember they had nibbled at the same grass and the same prickly thorn hedge, had ambled slowly round the same farm buildings, had scratched their sides and heads against the same tree and had stood nattering together for hours with their chins resting on the same gate. And their conversation was usually about the same thing.

"The grass was rather limp and tasteless this morning, didn't you think?" murmured the ewe one morning as they stood rubbing their chins against the rough wooden bar of the gate.

"I thought it was just the same as it was yesterday, and the day before, and the day before that," replied the nanny-goat, "and just the same as it always will be."

"There's nothing for it," said the ewe, "we shall have to go away for a holiday."

Now this is what the two old ladies had been deciding upon at this very spot for the past few years. So this particular occasion would have been nothing extraordinary if the nanny-goat had not replied unexpectedly, "All right, then. Let's pack up our things and go."

There was a short pause before the ewe turned timidly to her companion, who she knew was much the cleverer of the two, and said,

"You usually say 'All right, we'll do that one day.'"

"But I've been saying that for years, my dear, and we've never done anything about it," said the nanny-goat. "Whenever I look into the pond now I have to face the fact that I am not a kid any more. If we are ever going to take our holiday we must make a move now."

"This very minute?" asked the ewe, her large vacant eyes growing even wider.

"This very minute," replied the nanny-goat, "After all, my dear, we are neither of us getting any younger."

The ewe was a little doubtful about this sudden decision, but the nanny-goat had always known best and if she thought the time had come for a change, then she must be right. "We'll just go and collect our things, then," agreed the ewe, mildly.

It was only as they were walking back to their corrugated iron shed that they remembered that they really hadn't got any things to collect. All they had ever needed was grass to eat, and grass, as they perfectly well knew, grows everywhere, and so there was no point in taking any with them on their holiday. This thought made the ewe a little sad.

"Our first holiday," she murmured, "and I haven't anything new to take away with me."

The practical nanny-goat was very tolerant with her aged

friend and tried to cheer her up by saying, "We shall have to borrow something from the farmhouse. After all, we are coming back in a little while and we can return it then."

So they strolled slowly, side by side, to the door of the farmhouse, where they paused to make sure that no one was about. Apart from tables and chairs there didn't seem much at first glance that could be taken away. But then the nanny-goat noticed a very large shopping bag.

"Would you like to borrow that to go away with?" she asked the ewe kindly.

"Oh, yes please," bleated the ewe, her voice quavering as much from age as from excitement. "And something to put in it, just a little something."

Her eyes travelled slowly upwards from the scrubbed kitchen table and rested on a shot-gun and a stuffed wolf's head hanging on the wall.

"I should think that *they* would be very nice to have," she said.

Very quickly for her years the nanny-goat clambered on to the table, removed the gun and the head and popped them into the big bag. And before anybody could notice them, the two old ladies had pushed and pulled each other and the bag through a hole in the hedge which they had known about for years and years.

They made slow progress, of course, because they were eating grass all the time as they went along. It certainly tasted fresher and sweeter than the farmyard grass. After a few hours they looked up in some surprise to find that they had actually nibbled their way into the forest.

"It is quite dark, my dear, and rather chilly in this forest," said the ewe, who was on the nervous side by nature.

"Don't worry," her companion reassured her. "I think I can hear voices and see something moving just ahead of us. Whoever it is will no doubt tell us where we can sleep comfortably. Perhaps they are tourists like ourselves."

And so the two elderly animals browsed their way on ivy and dark undergrowth until they came to the place where they had heard all the noise. They were terribly alarmed when they looked up and saw that they had walked into the middle of a pack of lean gray wolves.

"Welcome, ladies," cried the leader of the wolves, a hungry light glinting in his eye. "We are indeed delighted to be honored with your presence. In fact, we were just planning dinner." At this point he chuckled and dug his bony elbow into the ribs of the nearest wolf, who also chuckled. In no time the whole pack was chuckling and chortling while the two farmyard animals stood in the middle of them, quivering with fear.

But, as I said before, the goat was a clever old creature and the ewe was not going to panic until her friend made it quite clear that all was lost. In as steady a voice as she could manage in the circumstances the nanny-goat said to the wolf leader, "It is very kind of you, gentlemen, to offer us food, but I'm afraid we are on a diet at the moment. However, we should be delighted to sit down and share our food with you, if it is to your taste." And feeling a little more confident now that she had begun, she turned to her companion and asked, "What have we in our bag?"

With quivering hooves the ewe rummaged about in the bottom of the large bag and finally dragged out the stuffed wolf's head which she held up for all to see.

"No, no," said the nanny-goat, "that is much too fat to offer to our friends. There must be something better than that."

The ewe put the head back into the bag and poked about again before bringing it out for a second time. "This?" she asked, in a trembling voice.

"Good heavens, no, my dear," replied the nanny-goat. "We must have had that one for at least three or four days. What would the gentlemen think of us if we offered them that. No, there must be something fresher in there. I must apologize, gentlemen, for my companion."

The ewe put the head into the bag again and peered in after it. Then she put in one foot and scraped about for a little while before pulling out the head again. "This, then?" she asked.

"Now that is much more like it," said the nanny-goat, turning to the wolves and smiling. "That is what I call a really juicy fresh head. Can you find six or seven more like that in the bag?"

The ewe had no time to reply. There was an ear-splitting howl and the wolves fled into the depths of the forest, frightened out of their wits. Exchanging glances of relief and pride the ewe and nanny-goat ambled off in search of somewhere to spend the night.

The wolves had been running a long time when they at last found their path blocked by the large figure of a bear.

"Why are you all running like that?" asked the bear. "Is there a fire in the forest?"

In no time the leader of the wolves, having silenced all the other wolves who were eager to tell their version of the story, had explained everything to the bear. The bear thought for a moment and then licked his lips. "Hmm," he said, "if these farmyard animals live only on wolves' heads, then however fierce they are a bear is safe. Can't we come to an arrangement? You show me where I can find them. I'll catch them and we'll share the prize."

"Yes," agreed all the wolves at once, "we'll take you to them."

"They can't have got far," said the leader. "They're terribly old."

In no time the whole howling pack had turned round and was racing back in the direction of the ewe and the nanny-goat. The poor old bear was having great difficulty in keeping up with them. As they sped on making their fearful noise many of the little animals of the forest were driven in fright before them.

Soon the ewe and the nanny-goat, still ambling along side by side, were overtaken by a number of squealing squirrels.

"Whatever is the matter?" asked the ewe, beginning to feel very frightened again. "Is there a fire in the forest?"

"No," replied a squirrel, flashing past. "The wolves are back. Up a tree quickly."

The ewe and the nanny-goat stopped and looked blankly at each other. After a while the ewe said, "Up a tree? But we can't climb trees. Sheep and goats don't climb trees, at least, not at our age."

"All the same," replied the nanny-goat, "it is the last place they would think of looking for us, and we certainly can't run faster than the wolves. I think it may be our only hope. Hold on to the bag and I'll help you up."

And so they pushed and pulled each other into the very lowest branches of the nearest tree. The goat, who had always been the more agile of the two, managed to get a little higher and to find a rather safer perch than the unfortunate ewe, who felt herself in great danger of slipping down.

Soon their hearts began to beat faster as the wolves and the bear, who was panting very hard by this time, took up their positions around that very tree. The bear sat down immediately beneath the ewe and wiped his brow with a large shaggy paw. He gasped for breath a few times and then addressed the eager wolves.

"Well, as I see it there isn't much point in all keeping together now," he said, taking a deep breath in between every word, "so you chaps spread out and search the undergrowth while I sit here and organize things." The wolves knew that

he only wanted a rest, but since he was going to catch the fierce ewe and nanny-goat for them they let him have his own way and spread out.

Above him, in the tree, the old ewe was beginning to lose her hold. Desperately clutching the bag in front of her, it was all she could do to cling to the branch, and the nanny-goat could see that she was slowly slipping down farther and farther and that one of her back legs was dangling immediately above the head of the bear. He felt something brush his ear and absentmindedly put up his paw to flick it away. The goat held her breath. The moment had come. In a frantic effort to stop herself falling the ewe let the bag slip from her grasp.

The shot-gun, which until now they had quite forgotten about, slipped out of the falling bag, bounced on the ground behind the dozing bear and went off with a deafening "BANG!" And as it did so the nanny-goat cried at the top of her voice, "There's a bear! Set the dogs loose!"

The bear was never very conscious of what had happened. All he knew was that he was in some sort of danger, and away he fled, with the terrified pack of howling wolves close behind.

The goat clambered to the ground and helped her trembling companion down. Very relieved to be safe and sound still, they made their way together out of the forest. By dawn they had arrived back at the farm.

They still nibble at the same dry grass, rub their sides against the same tree and carry on their never-ending conversation at the gate. But now they really have got something to talk about.

Story Five

THE HERON AND THE CRANE

Once upon a time, in a bog, there lived a heron and a crane. They didn't live together—the heron had built her scrappy nest on a dry mound at one end of the bog and the crane had built his, which looked exactly the same, at the other end.

One day, as the crane was standing and gazing at himself in the shallow, muddy water, it occurred to him that he was rather lonely. He scratched the back of his left leg with his right foot for a while, and then said to himself, "It is high time that I got married. . . . But to whom?" It didn't take him long to decide that he should marry the heron, because she was the only unmarried bird who was roughly the same shape and size as he was. There were some spinster sedge warblers, but they were out of the question.

And so, after cleaning himself very carefully, the crane stepped gracefully through the still water until he came to the other end of the bog where the heron was sitting on her nest.

"Good morning, heron," said the crane, feeling a little embarrassed, because, although he had been thinking hard as he walked along, he still hadn't quite decided how to phrase his proposal.

"Good morning, crane," replied the heron, who had no idea why he was visiting her. "Won't you come in?" She stood up and took a step backwards to make room for him to stand

on the edge of her nest. She didn't invite him to sit down with her as there wasn't enough room for all the legs.

"Will you marry me?" asked the crane suddenly. He had meant to lead up to this subject rather gradually, but in his excitement he couldn't think of anything else to say.

Naturally, the heron was very taken aback—she just wasn't prepared for a proposal of marriage at such short notice. And so we can't really blame her for losing her head a little and crying, "Marry you! Goodness gracious, what a ridiculous idea! Just look at you—you are all legs and neck! And those awful knobbly knees!"

The crane was very surprised by this outburst. He cast a sad look over his shoulder at his knees—they *were* rather bony.

"And what's more, you just couldn't keep me in fish!" She shouted this so loudly, that he knew it was time to go. Without a backward glance he turned and made his way slowly through the bog to his own nest at the other end.

When he had disappeared from view the heron thought it over again and was very unhappy about the way she had behaved. It was very, very unkind, she thought, to have insulted him like that, and as for the fish, well, she was perfectly capable of catching her own. When she had reasoned this out to herself, she made up her mind to take a stroll to the other end of the bog, apologize and offer to marry the crane.

She left her nest and picked her way gracefully through the bog water, hanging down her head very coyly as she approached the crane's nest. The crane was standing sulkily with his back to her, but it was obvious that he had heard her coming.

"Crane!" she called softly.

He didn't answer.

"Crane!" she called again, a little louder. "I've come to apologize. I don't really think all those nasty things I said, and I take them all back."

He didn't move.

"Crane, I should be happy to become your wife."

On hearing this the crane turned round and gave her a stony stare. "Thank you very much for your kind offer," he said, "but, as you remarked previously, I don't want an extra beak to feed. Marriage between us is out of the question."

There was a moment of complete silence over the bog before the heron burst into floods of tears and hurried off back to her own nest.

When she was out of sight the crane thought it all over to himself and became very miserable. "Why was I so cruel?" he thought. "I want to marry her, and now I've hurt her feelings. There's nothing for it, I shall have to pay her a visit and apologize for my behavior."

He really did feel very sorry for what he had said, and to ease his conscience he caught a juicy frog which he carried dangling by one leg from the end of his beak. He stepped hastily through the bog and stopped a little way from the heron's nest. He was so agitated that the frog was quivering.

"Heron," he mumbled nervously, "I am sorry for what I said a little while ago, and I have brought you this ..."

The heron didn't give him time to finish. Her pride had been hurt and now she was in quite a temper. "I don't want your pity, you fickle bird!" she boomed. "I know your sort.

I would rather remain alone until the end of my days than marry someone as hard-hearted as you!"

This wasn't the welcome the crane had expected. His beak half opened in dismay and the frog fell with a soft plop into the wet mud.

"This is the end, then," he thought to himself, and turned to make his way back to the other end of the bog.

When he had gone, the heron thought to herself, "How sad he looked. I think I must have punished him too severely. I do so want to marry him. What if he should do something terrible! Why, he may even throw himself into the bog and drown himself!"

This was rather a fanciful idea as the bog was nowhere more than four inches deep and the crane was a rather large bird. But it was enough to terrify the heron. She almost ran to the other end of the bog to convince herself that the crane was still alive.

When she arrived she gasped breathlessly, "Oh, crane, so you are safe! Forgive a foolish bird for her past ..."

The crane interrupted her, "Oh, I've seen these moods before. One minute you're as meek as a water vole and the next you're screeching your head off at me. No thank you ..."

And before he could finish she had turned and walked away, back to her own nest at the other end of the bog.

There is really no need to say that the crane very soon thought things over. But, of course, the heron wouldn't have him. And so they went on, day in day out, backwards and forwards from one end of the bog to the other. They are probably still at it now.

Story Six

THE KITTEN AND THE VIXEN

One day the vixen was walking slowly through the forest feeling rather miserable because the wolf and the bear had been teasing her as usual and threatening to bite off her beautiful red tail. She was so busy with her thoughts that she didn't notice that somebody was standing in her path, and was quite surprised to hear a voice ask, "Please may I have my dinner, now?"

She was even more surprised to look down and see that the question had come from a very, very small kitten, who was looking up at her with big round green eyes. Of course, the vixen didn't know that it *was* a kitten, because cats don't live in forests as a rule and she had never been out of the forest. At first she was rather suspicious of the furry little stranger, and backed away nervously, sniffing in his direction as she did so. But he looked so small and harmless and he had asked his question so politely, that she was sure that he couldn't really be a dangerous animal.

"Who are you?" she asked in return. "And what dinner might that be?" she added because she was rather inquisitive.

"I'm a kitten. My name is Tibbles and I'm five weeks old. You have to put my food down for me five times a day until I get a bit bigger. Little and often. May I have it now, please?"

The vixen was quite touched by the kitten's manner, it was so different from the impoliteness of the wolf and the bear, and she wanted to help him if she could. And so she asked, "What do you have for dinner?"

"Haven't you ever kept a kitten before?" asked Tibbles, who believed that everyone knew all about kittens.

"No," said the vixen sadly. "I've always been too poor. But I have an idea. If you agree to a plan which is forming in my mind, then you and I will have as much dinner as we want, whenever we want."

"That sounds very nice," said the kitten. "I shall want it five times a day until I'm a bit bigger. What have I got to do?"

"Well, I think we should get married," said the vixen excitedly, for she had been leading a very lonely life.

"But I'm only five weeks old!" protested the kitten. But when he saw how sadly her beautiful brush drooped at these words, he changed his mind and agreed. "All right, then," he said. "But you've got to give me my dinner."

And so the vixen walked slowly and proudly back to her earth with her new husband bouncing along beside her, purring happily at the thought of food.

Although her main reason for marrying the kitten had been because she liked him, the vixen was a very clever animal and was chewing over a special plan. The next morning, having made sure that her husband was dozing comfortably after his breakfast, the vixen trotted out into the heart of the forest.

Just as she had expected, it wasn't very long before she was met by the bear and the wolf, who immediately began to tease her.

"Why, wolf, what a beautiful tail the young lady is wearing! Don't you think it would look rather fine on me," chuckled the bear.

"Perfect!" said the wolf. "Why don't you try it for size?"

And the two ill-mannered animals bounded around the vixen, who stood her ground remarkably calmly, until the bear's soft, wet nose came within reach of her paw. And then, suddenly, she cuffed it with all her might. The bear sat down suddenly with tears trickling down his snout. It was all most unexpected. Bears are very large animals and vixens, as a rule, just don't hit them. Before he had a chance to protest, or the wolf could avenge his friend, the vixen began to speak,

"Gentlemen, in the past you have always treated me very badly. Now that Tibbles, lord and master of the forest and all that lives in the forest, has condescended to take me for his wife, it goes without saying that all that will change. Please do not think me weak-willed simply because I have gone down on my bended knees before Tibbles in order to beg him to spare you for your past behavior. Make no mistake about it. If you ever give me cause to change my mind, Tibbles will be pleased to eat both of you!" And she drew herself up to her full height and glared at them.

Since they were both rather cowardly, they didn't know whether to believe her or not.

"I don't know any animal in the forest that is bigger than I am," said the bear. "Or has sharper teeth than I have," added the wolf.

The vixen looked scornful. "How can you talk about size. As if that mattered. Tibbles, I would have you know, is no ordinary animal of the forest. Tibbles come from the town, and what is more, has to be fed five times a day!"

The wolf and the bear exchanged looks of amazement. "In that case, perhaps we had better come along and meet this new lord of the forest," said the bear, who was feeling very guilty about his treatment of the vixen in the past.

"Meet him!" exclaimed the vixen, "before you have made him the usual present of food! That would be asking for trouble!" And she went on to explain how the normal custom was to place great piles of the very best food the forest offered in front of the forest lord's earth, before one could be presented to him.

On hearing this, the bear and the wolf scuttled off together to collect the most delicious food they could find, while the vixen trotted off to her earth to prepare the kitten for the part he had to play.

Later that day, the bear and the wolf crept cautiously towards the vixen's home, stopped several yards in front of the entrance and placed on the ground all the food which they had brought with them: the carcass of an ox, lots of mutton and piles of sweet-smelling fruit. When they had done this they tiptoed into the bushes. The bear called softly to a passing hare, who came over to see what he wanted.

"Be a good fellow," said the bear, "and deliver a message for us at the vixen's earth. All you have to say is, 'The wolf and the bear pay their respects to the great Tibbles, lord of the forest, and offer him this small present of food.' And having said that, run for all you're worth!" The hare was puzzled, but agreed to deliver the message, which he did, watched all the time by the bear and the wolf. They had dug a little hiding-place for themselves in the undergrowth and had covered themselves with leaves, so that although they could watch Tibbles at his food, they could not be seen.

Slowly Tibbles strolled out of his new home. He stopped and gazed at the enormous mountain of meat and fruit in front of him. It was much too much for a kitten, he knew, but the vixen had explained everything that he had to do very carefully, so he wasn't worried. With great difficulty he began to clamber on to the carcass of the ox.

"It's rather small to be lord of the forest, isn't it?" asked the bear in a whisper, but the wolf quickly put his paw over the bear's mouth.

"Do be careful," he whispered back through chattering teeth, "or he will hear you!" This thought frightened the bear into silence.

By this time Tibbles had reached the top of the carcass, and had begun to lick it rapidly with his little tongue. He would have chewed it a bit but it hadn't been started and he was used to having his meat cut up for him. After a while he looked up, made the most dissatisfied expression he could manage, and said,

"Not enough! This isn't enough. I want more! More!"

In their hiding-place the wolf and the bear were both terrified to hear these words. In fact, the wolf was so nervous that he began to quiver, and the quivering of his snout set the leaves around him a-quivering, and the quivering leaves

made a rustling noise which the sharp ears of the kitten heard immediately. All at once he forgot that he was being lord of the forest, and to the horror of the vixen, who was watching from her earth, he crouched down in his mouse-watching position. He was absolutely certain that there was a mouse in the bushes.

"We didn't give him enough to eat," gasped the bear, "and now he is going to punish us!"

At that moment the kitten sprang at his imaginary mouse. As his little claws sank into the noses of the bear and the wolf, the two animals leapt up from the hiding-place, turned tail and fled into the heart of the forest.

The vixen trotted out to collect her puzzled husband.

"Did I do it right?" he asked.

"Yes," she replied with a satisfied smile on her face. "From now on I think we shall have plenty to eat."

"And I'm only five weeks old, too," said the kitten.

Since that day the bear and the wolf, and many other animals of the forest, have placed their gifts at the earth of the vixen and her husband. And whenever the happy pair take a stroll through the forest, the other animals are careful to keep out of their way.

THE JUNGLE BAND

It was a very hot afternoon in the jungle and a sloth and a gibbon, for want of anything better to do, were idly gossiping in the branches of a tall tree. The sloth was hanging head down, clasping the branch with all his four feet, while the gibbon, grasping a slightly higher branch with one long arm, swayed gently backwards and forwards in front of him.

Suddenly a small warthog burst out of the thick undergrowth and trotted daintily to the foot of the tree. He looked up eagerly to see if there were any animals about and at once caught sight of the sloth and the gibbon hanging together like a cluster of hairy fruit way up among the leaves. The warthog was obviously very excited about something. Clearly he had some news to tell, and simply could not wait to tell it.

"Gibbon! Sloth!" he called, jumping up and down impatiently. "Do come down here. I've something important to tell you."

"Couldn't you come up here and tell us?" asked the sloth, not because he wasn't interested in hearing the news, but simply because he was very slow and lazy by nature and hated the thought of having to leave his present comfortable position.

"You know I can't climb trees," squealed the little warthog. "Please, come down. Hurry."

The gibbon was curious to know what the interesting news might be about, and leapt from branch to branch, swinging lower and lower as he went, until he landed at the feet of the warthog.

"Well, what is it?" he asked, his big, round eyes bulging with expectation.

"I'll tell you when the sloth comes down," replied the warthog, who didn't want to have to tell his story twice.

It took a long time for the sloth to reach the lowest branch from where he could hear what the warthog was saying. He moved so slowly and stopped so often, just as if he were falling asleep. The two animals at the foot of the tree had to keep reminding him that he was coming down to hear some good news. At long last, as I said, he reached the lowest branch and hung there, with his eyes half closed.

"Now tell us the news," pleaded the gibbon, waving his long arms above his head in excitement.

"Well," began the warthog, "we have a new animal in this part of the jungle. He is called a mongoose. He is about this long, with feet like that and a head like this." The warthog indicated what the mongoose looked like by holding up his front trotters as he spoke.

"I see," said the gibbon. "You mean a gibbon with short arms and a tail."

"Yes, yes," said the sloth. "A sloth, only up the wrong way."

Satisfied that the two animals had now got some idea about the mongoose, the warthog went on, "And the important thing is that ever since he was a very small mongoose he has lived in a house, with human beings!"

The other two animals whistled in amazement. The gibbon brought one hand over to scratch the top of his head, and the sloth's eyes were now fully open, which meant that he was really excited.

"You mean to say that he has escaped?" he gasped.

"Won't he have some stories to tell!" chattered the gibbon.

"Let's go off and find him," suggested the warthog. "He's a good chap by all accounts and will almost certainly tell us about his experiences in a cage."

The sloth gave a low moan. It had taken him much effort to get to the bottom of the tree and he couldn't bear the thought of having to move again so soon. However, he needn't have worried because at that very moment the mongoose himself appeared from the bushes.

"What a long nose for a gibbon," thought the gibbon.

"What short toes for a sloth," thought the sloth.

But, of course, they all said "Good afternoon" very politely and soon they were deep in conversation about the mongoose's past life.

"You poor thing," said the warthog sympathetically. "What a hard time you must have had."

"How glad you must be to have escaped," added the gibbon.

The mongoose looked a little surprised. "It wasn't like that at all," he said. "I had a very enjoyable time, and I didn't escape —I simply thought I would like a change."

The other animals stared, scarcely able to believe their ears, and so he continued.

"You see, I had a pretty important job in the house. I was the chief snake-catcher. I got paid handsomely for doing it too. They gave me all the food I wanted and my time was my own. I was officially known as a 'pet'—that means that everybody had to obey me and see that I had all that I wanted. Life, of course, was much more exciting in the house than it is in the jungle. Why, practically every week there was a party, with dancing and a band."

"It sounds great fun," said the sloth, a little enviously. "Why don't we have a band?"

"Yes, indeed!" cried the warthog. "Why didn't we think of it before. A band. A band of our very own."

"What is a band?" asked the gibbon.

Seeing that the other two animals didn't know either, the mongoose began to explain as best he could.

"Well, it is a small group of people ..."

"... or animals?"

"... or animals," he continued, "who play together on musical instruments."

And then, noticing the blank looks on their faces, he went on,

"They scrape, blow or bang pieces of wood and things, to make a pleasant noise."

The other animals agreed that it sounded wonderfully exciting and were eager to form themselves into a band on the spot.

"But we haven't got the pieces of wood which you were talking about," said the warthog.

"Never mind," replied the mongoose. "I will describe them to you and by tomorrow you will have found or made them. First we will need a violin. You, gibbon, have the most elegant arms, and so you shall play the violin." And he went on to explain to the attentive gibbon how the violin and bow could be made from a piece of wood, a stick and some creeper.

The mongoose continued, "You, warthog, because you are so good at jumping up and down, shall play the drum, and you, sloth, because you have such good lungs (what he really thought was 'because you have no hands to spare, since you hang like that all the time') shall play the clarinet." And he described these instruments and explained how they could be made from a hollow tree stump with tough leaves stretched over it and from a hollow cane with holes punched in it.

"Then," said the mongoose, "we shall need a conductor. The conductor is the most important one, really. He stands in front and sees that everything is done properly."

There was a moment's silence, and then the gibbon had an idea, "Why not you? You could be conductor."

The other two agreed wholeheartedly, and at last the blushing mongoose gave in and consented to be conductor.

"We must meet here at the same time tomorrow," he said, "with instruments." And saying a cheery "Good-bye" he disappeared into the bushes.

"I think it sounds exciting," said the warthog, "having a band of our own."

"And to think that that is what living in a house is like," said the sloth. "I always imagined that you had to work terribly hard" (here he shuddered at the very thought of working) "and had very little food for your pains."

"In fact," said the gibbon, "I am seriously thinking of leaving the jungle and taking up a job as a pet somewhere."

This idea struck the others as being very sensible after what they had heard from the mongoose and they discussed it all the time as they rummaged among the branches and the grass for material for their instruments.

The next afternoon at the same time they were in the same places eagerly awaiting the arrival of the mongoose. He appeared from the bushes again carrying a stick.

"That's a nice instrument," said the sloth. "Do you scrape, bang or blow it?"

The mongoose explained that it was a baton and that the conductor had to wave it in front of the band. Then he looked about him at their home-made instruments. Quite honestly he was a little disappointed after the trouble he had taken to describe them so exactly, because they didn't really look anything like the instruments he had seen at the house. But he was a good-natured mongoose and didn't want to spoil their fun, so he said nothing.

"May we begin?" wheezed the sloth, who was finding the clarinet clenched between his teeth rather uncomfortable, and anyway he was anxious to start before he fell asleep.

"Yes," began the mongoose, "I think we are ready to ..."

Before he could finish the animals had started to scrape, bang and blow at their instruments for all they were worth. The jungle had never heard such a terrible din. After a minute or two they stopped and looked enquiringly at the mongoose. He couldn't pretend that it sounded like music, and so he said,

"I should have explained, you have to watch me. The band always watches the conductor. Go."

Again they struck up the same ear-splitting noise, scraping, banging and blowing with all their might. After another minute or two they again stopped and looked at the mongoose.

"I know what the trouble is," he said. "You are all in a straight line. You have to be in a half-circle around me. That was how they used to do it at the house."

The animals changed their positions willingly—they wanted the music to be as nice as possible. Then they started again. Animals at the other end of the jungle began howling as the terrible sounds reached their ears. Once more the playing came to a stop.

The mongoose looked extremely puzzled. "The sounds seem to be better now," he said, "but they aren't quite ... together. Perhaps you should move closer to each other. That's it. The people in the bands at the house always sit very close together. That's what has been wrong."

The animals shifted their positions again and played—with the same awful results. The mongoose suggested that they should play with the shortest on the right and the tallest on the left. So they did. Then he suggested that they should try with the tallest on the right and the shortest on the left. They did that, too. Then they played sitting down (except the sloth) and then they even exchanged instruments (except the sloth) and each time the noise was even worse than before.

"Well," said the mongoose, looking very downcast "I think we have practised enough for the first time. We are getting much better, you can tell," he forced himself to say politely. And with that he said good-bye and slipped away into the bushes.

The other animals looked at each other, wondering who would speak first. At last the gibbon reached out an arm, put down his instrument and scratched his chin.

"I've been thinking it over," he said. "Being a pet is all very well. It is a good job to have, very important and all that, and yet—I don't think I could stand the noise."

The others nodded their heads, the warthog in agreement, the sloth because he was falling asleep. The mongoose did not come back the next day. They later heard that he had returned to his house. The warthog, the sloth and the gibbon just couldn't understand why.

First published in 1960 by Faber and Faber Limited

This edition published in 2017 by Thames & Hudson Ltd
in association with House of Illustration

www.thamesandhudsonusa.com

Library of Congress Control Number 2017934849

ISBN 978-0-500-65135-3

Printed and bound in China by C & C Offset Printing Co. Ltd